A Leaf on the Wind

A Collection of Tanka Poetry

Brett C. Persson

A Leaf on the Wind
A Collection of Tanka Poetry

www.brettcpersson.com

@BrettCPersson

Cover Art and Illustrations

by S.C. Persson

scpersson.art

Nudous Publishing, LLC

www.nudouspublishing.com
info@nudouspublishing.com

Paper ISBN: 978-1-964793-87-0

Dedication

This is for my family, who I love dearly but may not always show. Thank you for always being there for me, even when I was at my lowest. The encouragement and forgiveness you have demonstrated over the years is remarkable.

Bev, Ray, Kim, Kinsey, Sara, Baylie, Jeff, & Trish

Thank you, and I love you all.

I am a leaf on the wind; watch how I soar.

… Hoban Washburne

Table of Contents

Nature

1

Waves Break On The Shore

The White Sands Briefly Covered

Water Soon Recedes

Water Never Returning

But Moving On Somewhere Else

2

The Snow Falls Outside

Collects On The Windows Ledge

It Builds And Mounds Up

Winter Wind Blows, And It Goes

Sent Adrift Into The Air

3

Blooming Flowers Grow

Rain Dampens The Fertile Grass

Spring Has Sprung To Life

Rejuvenating Nature

The World Is Reborn Again

4

Clouds Filled With Cold Rain

Wet And Ready To Release

Dropping From The Sky

Down To Thirsting Mother Earth

Water Is The Source Of Life

5

The Meadow Is Green

The Sky Is A Baby Blue

The Dirt Is Chestnut

The Clouds Are White Mixed With Gray

People's Color Matters Not

6

The Tree Creaks Softly

It Bends Under The Moon's Glow

Tilting Back And Forth

Swaying In The Night's Darkness

Holding Strong With Its Deep Roots

7

The Bird Hatches Free

Born To World Of Future Flight

Momma Feeds Baby

Quick Grows Does The Baby Bird

Soon Pushed From The Nest To Fly

8

Trees With Twisted Roots

Trunks Covered In Moss And Vines

Canopy Massive

Old, Tall, Strong Reaching Up, Out

Standing In Spite Of Mankind

9

Oceans Of The Deep

Pressure So Fierce And Mighty

Blocking Out The Light

Little Life Able To Live

Creatures Unknown To Humans

10

Ground Starts To Rumble

Magma Working To Surface

Lava Reaching Out

Explosion Erupts Fiercely

Ash Plume Sprays High, Lava Flows

11

A Violent Swirl

Rotating Column Of Air

The Finger Of God

Destroys Anything In Path

Laying Waste And Destruction

12

Hearing The Rain Fall

Peaceful, Calming, Relaxing

Laying In The Dark

Hearing Nature So Profound

Letting Worries Wash Away

13

Leaves Fall From The Sky

Floating Down With No Purpose

Free To Fall And Land

Meeting Ground Without Purpose

Just What They Do When They Fall

14

It Lands On My Foot

It Tickles Me As It Walks

A Fly Exploring

Seeing What The World May Hold

Apparently, It Likes Me

15

Sun So Bright It Hurts

Laying In A Green Meadow

Enjoying The Rest

The Warmth And Peace Flooding In

Perfect Summer Day Enjoyed

16

The White Capped Mountain

Holds The Little Wood Cabin

A Nice Fire Burning

Relaxing With Family

Free From Modern City Life

17

The Frog Leaps Across

It Sits On A Flat Warm Stone

He Ribbits And Blinks

He Sees A Fly Circle By

He Strikes Fast And Has His Lunch

18

A South Wind Blows In

Bringing In A Murky Storm

Cold, Wet, And Driven

Releasing The Life Water

Hydrating The Earth's Body

19

The Kitten Stretches

Protected By Her Momma

Waking From Her Nap

She Starts A New Day Carefree

The Adventure Of Her Life

20

In Forest Hunting

Foliage Is Thick And Dense

Searching For Fresh Game

Animals Provide For Clan

Wilderness Survivalist

21

River Flows Downstream

Rippling On The Timeworn Rocks

Always Running On

Water Never Stops To Think

Constantly Moving Onward

22

Lake Without Ripple

Enters Forest Silently

No Disturbance Felt

Calm Like A Blade Of Green Grass

She Goes With Grace And Respect

23

Wind Is Wild Like Life

Grass Is Green Along The Shores

The Sun Is Glowing

Here Is Where No Bull Can Hide

The Truth Open To Be Free

24

The Crisp Night Air Flows

The Harvest Moon Shining Bright

A Cold Autumn Night

An Unaccompanied Soul

Desolation Of Lost Love

25

Plunging Waterfalls

Glowing Lights In The North Sky

Deep Dense Rainforest

Life Building The Coral Reef

Endless Sands Of The Desert

26

Mountain Peak Of High

Chilling Breeze Of Frost And Snow

Air Too Thin To Breathe

Isolated, Abandoned

Seldom Visited By Man

27

The Great Mother Weeps

Of Man's Destruction And Waste

Shattering Her Soul

Slowly Dying In Silence

Unforgivable Damage

28

Staring At The Moon

Serene In Her Beauty

Dead, Cold, And Lifeless

Always A Dream In My Mind

To Go, To Live, To Be Free

29

I Stand In The Stream

Feeling The Water Flow By

Cool On My Worn Feet

Water Heals My Heart, My Soul

Needed Rest From My Travels

30

Nature Hurries Not

Will Last Longer Than Mankind

Resilient And Strong

Capable To Heal Itself

The True Source Of Existence

31

Blooming Red Flower

Lush Trees Growing Tall And Strong

Green Vines Stretching Out

Natural Beauty Of God

Life In The Purest Design

32

Swimming By The Reef

Seeing The Life Of The Sea

Animals Not Plants

Nature's Own Water Filter

Giving Life To The Water

33

Autumn In The Air

Feeling The Changing Season

Dawn Of A New Day

Chill Entering In The Night

Relief From The Hot Summer

34

A Path Through The Woods

Trees Building A Canopy

Shading The Journey

Giving Relief From The Sun

Absorbing Life From Nature

35

The Water Falls Down

Feeding The Large Lake Below

From Rocks High Above

Lake Flows Into The River

Making Way To The Ocean

36

The Wolf Hears The Call

Echoing In Mountain Pass

Senses Now Heightened

Predators Enter Their Space

The Enemy Known As Man

37

The Stream Of Life Flows

All Living Things In Nature

Is The Source Of Life

Water And Carbon, Life Base

The Cycle Of Life On Earth

38

Rain Hitting The Roof

As I Listen, I Relax

Calms My Anxious Mind

Natures Soothing Melody

Finally, I Can Find Sleep

Macabre

39

The Boat Has Succumbed

Lost In The Raging Ocean

Crew Fighting To Live

Screams Drowned Out By Loud Thunder

People Drown Scared And Alone

40

A Hardened Heart Closed

Shutoff From Love Of Others

Alone In Himself

A Choice Of Isolation

Choosing To Die Without Love

41

The Fire Starts So Small

It Soon Spreads Around The House

Alarms Start To Ring

People Begin To Awake

Fleeing Raging Inferno

42

He Feels The Pain Surge

Feels It Going Down His Arm

His Chest Is So Tight

Blackness Invades His Vision

Death Stands Above Him Waiting

43

Man Filled With Hatred

Rising To Power Unstopped

Slaughtering The Jews

Crazed With Hunger For Power

Finally Stopped By The Brave

44

Car Skidding Through Snow

Out Of Control On Black Ice

Going Off The Road

Spin Across The Median

Stopped By A Semi, All Dead

45

Wars From Days Of Old

History Painted In Blood

Innocent Victims

Always Caught In The Middle

Dead Casualties Of War

46

Flowers On The Grave

Tears Fill Up His Old Tired Eyes

Sorrow In The Heart

Sixty Plus Years Together

He Hopes To Follow Her Soon

47

Twisted Deviant

Hunting Children Like A Sport

Pure Evil People

Should Only Suffer Long Death

Tortured By Their Parent's Rage

48

Trapped In A Foxhole

Two Brothers In Arms Fighting

Keeping Each From Harm

Bond Stronger Than Any Blood

Soldiers In A Frontline War

49

The Sun Always Sets

The Same As Life Ebbs Away

Cannot Fight And Win

Breath Eventually Fails

Heart Fails And Lungs Deflate, Death

50

She Feels So Hopeless

She Sees No Way Up Or Out

Totally Consumed

She Puts The Blade To Her Wrist

Fast And Deep, Decision Made

51

Weak From The Journey

A Lay Down In Green Pastures

My Soul Tired And Worn

I Seek True Understanding

But Hear Nothing But Silence

52

Wave Crashes Over

Swallow The Salty Water

My Head Dips Below

I Taste The Salty Water

My Lungs Burning As I Drown

53

Gun In His Pocket

He Enters The Bodega

Addiction Winning

Taking Away His Reason

Violence Feeding Habit

54

Panic In His Mind

Darkness Imprisoning Him

His Soul Lost To Dark

He Cannot Live, Cannot Die

Trapped In Endless Misery

55

Dearly Departed

We Gather Around The Grave

Ashes To Ashes

From The Earth, We Shall Return

Gone But Never Forgotten

56

The Water Trickles

Down His Weak Leg To His Feet

Fearful To The Core

A Gun Against His Forehead

Flash, Bang, Bullet Fires, Darkness

57

Lost In Confusion

Wandering The Streets At Night

Needle Still In Arm

Unaware Of Anything

Deadman Walking Last Steps

58

Feeling The Rush Hit

Pumping In Through The Veins

Another Step Down

Closing In, An Early Death

Not Caring, Not Worrying

59

Troops March In The Streets

Is It The Apocalypse

Worse Than That Ending

The Coming Of A Madman

The New Leader Of The Reich

60

Mankind Deeply Flawed

Hate Is Stronger Than Love Is

Hearts Are Cold And Dead

Conflict Easier Than Peace

Carnage Over Decency

61

November Eighteenth

Committed Mass Suicide

Jonestown Massacre

Settlement In Guyana

More Than Nine Hundred Souls Lost

62

Plane Soars Overhead

At Eight Forty-Six A.M.

About Floor Eighty

Shatters Through Concrete And Glass

America Changed That Day

63

Columbine Shooting

Ruby Ridge And Waco Siege

Trade Center Bombing

Operation Desert Storm

Noriega Surrenders

64

Left Without A Trace

Vanished From The Street At Night

Seeking To Find Her

First Forty-Eight Nearly Gone

Desperation Setting In

65

A White Powder Line

Taken From The Purest Source

Deadly Addictive

Euphoria Washes In

Problems Seem To Melt Away

66

Lips Taste Of My Blood

My Ribs Broken And Shattered

Laying In A Heap

The Fall Stopped By The Hard Ground

Final Resting Place For Me

67

Under Overpass

Newports And A Fifth Of Jack

Cold And Rainy Night

A Life Derailed Long Ago

Failed To Rebuild The Pieces

68

Feeling Grief Of Loss

I Sit Alone In The Dark

Wondering What's Next

Hard To Imagine The Loss

A Part Of Me Dies As Well

Hope, Joy, and Love

69

The Wind Blows Her Hair

Summer Sun Shines On Her Face

Grass Beneath Her Feet

Love Feeding Her Joyful Soul

A Life Worth Living In Peace

70

Running And Playing

Leaping And Chasing Around

Energy Abounds

Quickly Wearing Themselves Out

They Are My Girls, My Puppies

71

She Smells Like The Spring

Her Smile Lights Up Like The Sun

She's My Light, My Hope

She Brings Out The Best In Me

She Makes Me A Better Man

72

What Has Come Before

Change Is On The Horizon

Things Always Changing

Nothing Remaining The Same

Life Evolving Around Us

73

The Young Puppies Play

Jumping, Leaping, and Rolling

Happy And Playful

Running Around Chasing Kids

The Gift Of Dogs On Our Life

74

Feeling Takes Over

The High That Can Consume Me

Powerless Was I

Found Sobriety In Rooms

Life's Doors Opened Once Again

75

Birth Of A Baby
A New Life Born In This World
Free From Life's Hatred
Will Only Last A Short Time
Knowledge Soon To Corrupt Soul

76

A Blanket Laid Out
Flowers And Chilling Champagne
Picnic Basket Full
The Ring Tucked In His Pocket
Hope In His Heart For A Yes

77

The Meaning Of Life

Striving For True Happiness

Avoid Suffering

Finding An Internal Peace

Content With One's Own Being

78

Chaos Is Not Wrong

It Is A State Of Being

Invention Of Thought

Ebbing And Flowing Conscience

Thinking Dynamically

79

Need No Barriers

Between You And Where You Are

Journey Has Begun

When Mind Is Free And Open

Body No Longer Required

80

Can't Easily Hide

You Put The Shine On The Sun

Sweetest Eyes Ever

You Are My Wonderful Life

Tell Everyone How I Feel

Religion

81

David Just A Man

A Mammoth Named Goliath

Big Man Mocked The Lord

David Takes On Goliath

Goliath Dead, Rock And Sling

82

A Flood Is Coming

Noah Prepares For The Rain

Builds A Boat To Live

Two By Two Animals Board

Saves Family And Future

83

A Chair Is To Sit

A Bed Is For Love And Sleep

Shoes Are For Walking

House Is Shelter From Nature

Soul Belongs To Loving God

84

In Exile From Home

Feeling The Pain Of Others

Tibetan Leader

Man Of Holiness And Peace

A Righteous And Loving Man

85

Touching The Heavens

Passing Through His Holy Gates

His Eternal Peace

His Grace For All Who Enter

Being With The King Of Kings

86

Religion Is Faith

Faithless Does Not Mean Heartless

Peace Without A God

Possible Without A Doubt

Respect From Both Sides Needed

87

Jesus Walks Downtown

Seeing The World Dad Has Made

He Stops For A Slice

Messiah Among People

Just Observing The Lost Herd

88

Man Wandering Blind

He Laid His Hands Upon Him

Restoring His Sight

The Stories Of Jesus Tell

Miracles From King Of Kings

89

Hearing The Wind Blow

It Comes From The Valley Floor

Loving Breath Of God

His Presence Found If Sought For

Indications Presented

90

How Do You Believe

Making Sense Of Religion

Not For Everyone

I Tried, But I Can't Trust It

Either You Do, Or You Don't

91

Satan's Minions

Osteen, Swaggart, Falwell, Hinn

Looking For A Buck

Not Men Of God, But Money

Do Not Be Fooled By Their Greed

92

See Those Who Believe

Do Not Judge Or Condemn Them

They Are Not Stupid

Neither Are Those Who Do Not

Respecting Each Other's View

93

Life Ebbing Away

Grateful For What His Life Was

His Soul Finding Peace

Dilated And Blurry Eyes

Still Sees His Lord And Savior

Life

94

Love Is Like Nature

Can Grow Strong And Bloom More Life

Or Withers And Dies

Unstable And Messy Thing

Brings Hope And Death Every Time

95

They Lie, Cheat, And Steal

Presidents Do Come And Go

All The Same Poison

Out For Their Own Special Groups

Never For Masses They Serve

96

The End Of The Maze
With All Of The Twists And Turns
Always Ends In Death
The Path Of The Maze Is Life
Always Choices To Decide

97

Money Has No Sin
People Bring Things Upon Them
Making Their Choices
Foolishly Blaming Others
Satan, God, Friends, And Their Foes

98

The First Responders

What Is Your Emergency

Putting Out The Fires

Running Into The Danger

Supplying Critical Aid

99

Body Politic

Rising Against Its Leader

Forming Together

Grown Tired Of Their Dictator

Overthrowing Injustice

100

Frog And Scorpion

The Tale Of A Betrayal

Cutting Off Our Nose

We Do It Time And Again

Hurt The Ones We Need Help From

101

I See The Flag Wave

Red And White, Blue Field With Stars

Proud For Which It Stands

Not Perfect, But It Is Home

Nowhere Else I Want To Be

102

The Wind In My Face

Gravity Pulling Me Down

Freefalling So Fast

Adrenalin Pumping Hard

No Fears, No Regrets, Just Free

103

People Everyday

Hearing Without Listening

Just Nodding Away

Talking With Nothing To Say

A Zombie In Today's World

104

A Homeless Lost Soul

Laying Down Under The Bridge

Hungry And Bone Cold

Struggling With Mental Illness

Humanity Tossed Aside

105

Children Taught To Hate

By Racists And Extremists

Poisoning A Child

Judging By Their Skin Color

Or The Uniform They Wear

106

He Stumbles, He Falls

Rises To His Feet Shaken

Quickly Clears His Head

Is Ready To Start Again

Boxer Wants To Win The Fight

107

Making Your Own Way

Will Take Everything You Got

Relying On Self

Working Hard For What You Want

Nobody Owes You Nothing

108

Vanilla Bean Ghee

Oil Of Coconut Added

Coffee Fresh And Hot

Blended To Smooth Perfection

Hot And Delicious Keto

109

His Finger Trembles

He Shrugs It Off As Fatigue

It Continues On

Comes And Goes As Months Go By

Parkinson's Slithering In

110

Lost In His Own Mind

His Thoughts No Longer His Own

A Mental Breakdown

Trauma And Sorrow Stricken

Unable To Move Past It

111

Better Than Before

A Freedom Earned Not Given

A New Direction

The New Government Installed

Opportunity Begins

112

The Street Lights Go On

The Music Loud And Latin

Dancing All-Around

It Is A Celebration

Her Fifteenth Birthday Party

113

Is Loud And Noisy

Two Sisters Working Same Line

One Operator

The Other A Packager

Working Together As Team

114

Politicians Lie

And Religious Leaders Too

Hypocrites Them All

Only Worried About Self

People Now Losing Their Faith

115

For My Vanity

To Feed My Own Self Ego

Making My Own Mark

Self-Assurance Of Self Worth

Living My Own Delusion

116

The Russian Madman

Invading The Ukraine Land

Crazy, Desperate

Failing In So Many Ways

Freedom Resisting The Bear

117

Hawaiian Shirt Cut

From My Back As I Wear It

Cutting And Laughing

Times Of My Youth Remembered

Always Brings Smile To My Face

118

Darkness In The Room

The Door Closes Silently

The Click Of The Lock

Fear Now Consuming Their Mind

Unknowing Of What To Come

119

A Life In The Books

Focused More On Knowledge Gain

Little Contact Made

Without Socialization

Locked Alone In Your Own Mind

120

Thorns Of A Red Rose

Pierce Our Skin Cause Us To Bleed

We Don't Notice It

We Carry On Unconcerned

No Beauty Without Some Pain

121

Building In Ruins

Decayed Over The Long Years

Void Of The Living

Abandoned And Deserted

Waiting For Fallout Decay

122

Rolling Hills Of Green

Houses Built In The Landscape

Smoke Through The Chimney

A Peaceful And Quiet Life

Soon Snuffed Out Of Existence

123

Generation Soft

Growing Weaker And Weaker

They Will Not Listen

Cowards In Their Safe Places

Time To Buck Up Buttercup

124

He Now Wears The Crown

Boy King Rises To The Throne

Innocent Leader

A Ruler Before His Time

Forced To Grow Sooner Than Thought

125

My Head Hurts And Aches

Hammer Pounding My Temples

Eyes Blurry And Strained

Darkness Is Only Relief

Praying It To Stop Or Death

126

I Sip My Cola

The Sun Warm And The Drink Cold

Refreshing Spring Day

Perfect Day Before Summer

Blistering Heat Soon Arrives

127

Penitentiary

Surrounded By Concrete Walls

Bars Pounded From Steel

Trapped In A Six-By-Six Box

Life Locked Up On The Inside

128

I See What I See

Hear What They Don't Want Me To

Hidden From Their Sight

I Lurk, Lost In The Shadows

Your Children Always See You

129

grandes ojos marrones

pelo largo y negro

linda sonrisa

celebrar quinceañera

toda la familia

130

Illusion Of Time

Is Incomprehensible

The Passage Of It

Just A Small Cosmic Second

In The Vastness Of It All

131

On The Ragged Edge

Secessionist Rebellion

Fighting The Last Stand

Escaping Brutal Leader

Freedom For The Alliance

132

A New Civil War

Brewing In The Freedom Lost

Two-Party Failure

Hypocrisy Of Leaders

Keeping Down Its Citizens

133

Hiding Who You Are

A Mask To Conceal The Hate

Quiet The Voices

Darkness That Engulfs The Soul

Fighting Natural Instinct

134

Helping The Homeless

Finding Shelter For Women

Mission To D.R.

Airborne Man Following God

Paragon Of A Father

135

The Tik Tok Brainwashed

Hypnotized Stupidity

Mindless Drones Watching

Dumb And Ignorant Posters

Killing Brain Cells Like A Drug

136

Stricken By Despair

Hiding Deep In A Bottle

Drinks His Soul Away

Not Yet Hitting The Bottom

Time Will Determine Outcome

137

Ends One Of Three Ways

Jail, Institution, Or Death

If Help Is Not Found

Addicts Helping Each Other

Recover From Addiction

138

An Old Lake Cabin

Weathered By The Storms And Time

Left Behind To Rot

Memories Hidden In Time

No One Left To Remember

139

I Hear The Clock Tick

Time Passing By While I Wait

In The Long Night Hours

Unable To Sleep Again

Awake Alone With Myself

140

Cities Laid To Waste

Destroyed By Putin's Missiles

Senseless War And Hate

The Death Of Innocent Souls

Attacked By Dreams Of The Past

141

Unions Of Days Past

Once Were Needed, But Not Now

Business Of Unions

Not The People But Money

Union Greed Splitting Workers

142

A.I. On The Rise

Integrating Into Life

Seeing Benefits

Fear Not The Sci-Fi Movies

Safe To Develop This Tech

143

Freedom, A Mindset

Prison, A Reality

The Screams Never Stop

Struggling Just To Live A Life

Remembering All The Past

144

Dying Like Embers

My Own Lies Are Always True

Living Delusion

Coming To Reality

Haze Of Drugs Dissipating

145

The Reaper Watches

The Dread In His Eyes And Soul

Death Waiting For Him

Lost In His Hidden Dark Place

Only Seeing One Way Out

146

Journey Of One's Self

Unique Path For Each Of Us

By Choices We Make

The Best Way We Can Manage

We Traverse This Thing Called Life

147

Now Past The Mid-Point

My Life Closer To The End

Farther From The Start

Each Day Closer To My Death

Still A Journey Left To Live

148

I Think So I Am

Being Of The Mind And Soul

Complex And Simple

Human Shell Ponders All Seen

Speck Of Sand Among Billions

149

Left, Right, Left, Right, Left

March As A Single Unit

Led By Their Sergeant

Moving Through The Harsh Landscape

Seeking Out The Enemy

150

I Long For The Stars

Probably Born Too Early

Out Of Reach For Me

Next Generation Will Soar

Option For Those Who Seek It

151

The Heart Is Heavy

Filled With Sadness And Regret

Possible Life Lived

Hindsight Always Unclouded

Imagining Of What-If

152

Mind Confined Within

Locked In A Prison Called Life

Seeking Ascension

Living Free From The Body

Higher Plane Of Existence

153

Nations Rise And Fall

Through The History Of Time

Littered With Bodies

Men Used As Pawns On A Board

Innocents Often Slaughtered

154

Born In Late August

The Mustang Man Vincent C.

Joking And Laughing

Playing Games And Sleeping Late

Always Out To Beat Victor

155

The Big Dion D.

Strong In The Mind And Body

Training And Teaching

Cultivating New Talent

Working Out In The Lobby

Space

156

Regolith Kicked Up

Eagle Landing For First Time

Neil And Buzz Ready

The Touchdown Light And Precise

Mankind's First Steps On The Moon

157

Out In The Blackness

Traveling The Stars Of Night

Feel The Engine Burn

Only Silence In The Black

Free From Earth's Rules And Judgement

158

The Kessler Syndrome

Collisional Cascading

A Chain Reaction

Possible To Destroy All

Space Becomes Unreachable

159

Astra On The Pad

The Launch After A Failure

No Tumbling This Time

Reach Orbit Delivery

A Player Reaching Orbit

160

Plane Starts Its Engines

It Moves Towards The Runway

Ready For Takeoff

The Engines Roar, Full Throttle

Soaring To The Open Sky

161

A Perfect Heaven

Great Science Fiction Novel

Nothing Is Better

Science Is My Religion

Space Is Where My Soul Will Live

162

S.L.S. Rolls Out

Four And A Half Mile Journey

Eleven Hour Trip

Almost Ready For A Launch

Delayed More Than A Decade

163

Clearing The Tower

Tearing The Air Asunder

Roar Of The Engines

Racing Towards The Blackness

The Falcon Soars Once Again

164

Buckled In The Seat

Countdown Approaching Near Launch

Living In The Black

Traveling To Space At Last

Making The Journey To Mars

165

The Regolith Stirs

As Landing Engines Ignite

Ten Meters To Go

Man Returns To Moon Surface

Visions Of Years Past Now Here

166

Raptor Two Engine

Bringing The Starship To Life

New SpaceX Model

Bringing Humans To The Moon

Future Mars Exploration

Everything Else

167

Jack O. Is In Charge

Leader Of The Other Three

Carter The Second

Daniel Is The Diplomat

Teal'c The Warrior Jaffa

168

Sinclair Is Transformed

Delenn Of The Grey Council

Sheridan Cheats Death

Ivanova Telepath

Garibaldi Chief And Friend

169

Kirk Is A Fighter

Picard Is A Diplomat

Janeway Lost For Years

Sisko On The Space Station

Archer Was First True Captain

170

Traveled Back They Did

Back To Nineteen Sixty-Nine

Caused By Solar Flare

Michael And Jennifer Clark

Helped The Hero's Return Back

171

Jackson Knew They Did

Landing On The Pyramids

Ships From Far Away

Denounced Archeologist

Redemption Found For Himself

172

In A Stretched Limo

On The Way To The Premier

Walking The Carpet

Hollywood Makes Such A Fuss

Over Inflated Egos

173

Live Long And Prosper

As The Humans Say, Up Yours

Big Damn Heroes, Sir

The Force Is Strong With This One

Damn It Jim; I'm A Doctor

174

Doctor And Time Lord

Tom Baker Was The Longest

Tardis Police Box

A Science Fiction Icon

Whittaker First Woman Doc

175

Maranda Is Lost

No Terraforming Event

Death Caused By The Pax

Planet In Burnham Quadrant

A Reaver Occupied World

176

Londo Makes A Deal

Shadows Move In The Darkness

For Centauri Prime

Seeking To Destroy The Narn

Striving To Restore Power

177

It Shimmers And Glows

An Event Horizon Made

Rippling Like Water

Worlds Await The Traveler

To Unknown Destinations

178

John Crichton, NASA

Experimental Mission

Living Ship Moya

Peacekeeper Aeryn Sun Joins

Fighting To Beat Scorpius

179

Jaffa Warrior

First Prime Of Lord Apophis

A Golden Tattoo

Leader Of The Rebellion

Fighting To Free His People

180

Rick And Shane Waiting

Speeding Felons On The Run

Car Flips And Rick Shot

Alone In The Hospital

Awakens To A Nightmare

181

Jasper In A Tree

Injured And Bound To Branches

Spear Wound In His Chest

His Life Holding By A Thread

The Black Panther Approaches

182

The Harsesis Child

A Child Born Of Flesh And Bones

A Child Of Two Hosts

Protected By Ancients

Born With The Hosts Memory

183

Speech Cannot Convey

Words Cannot Express All Things

Spirit Is Wordless

When Swayed By Words, One Is Lost

You Must Believe And Have Faith

184

They Cannot Teach Him

With What He Already Knows

His Mind Is Closed Off

High Walls To Protect Oneself

Emotions Cut And Severed

185

I Am A Cyborg

In Lower South Korea

But That Is Okay

Locked In Mental Hospital

Another Thinks He Steals Souls

186

It Is So Clear Now

Longer Time To Realize

Candlelight Is Fire

Meal Cooked A Longtime Ago

Is Immediately Known

187

The Spirit Is Freed

When The Mind Is Enlightened

Body Matters Not

A Child Lives In All Of Us

Embracing It Is The Task

188

Some Lightning Flashes

In One Blink Of Your Own Eyes

A Shower Of Sparks

Oversight Of True Seeing

Those Who Seek Oneness Find It

189

Station Five Miles Long

Port Of Call For Refugees

A Dream Given Form

To Prevent Another War

Was Our Last Best Hope For Peace

190

Fever Of Pac-Man

Goodbye, Farewell, And Amen

The Empire Strikes Back

Top Gun, Die Hard, Breakfast Club

Appetite For Destruction

191

O.J., Diana

Run Forrest Run, Titanic

Clinton-Lewinsky

The X-Files, Seinfeld, Roseanne

Harry Potter, Y2K

192

Walking With The Dead

Hidden Beneath Lifeless Skin

A Deadly Whisper

Blended In Among The Dead

Waiting To Strike Their Victim

193

Addison, Joe Blake

John McClane, Butch Coolidge, Jackal

Harry S. Stamper

David Dun, James Cole, Bruno

Remembering Bruce Willis

194

The Shields Cascading

Dilithium Crystals Low

Enemy Port Bow

Photon Torpedoes Offline

Destruction Of A Starship

195

He Runs In The Swamp

Traversing The Rocks And Roots

Damp, Foggy, Humid

Searches For Understanding

Rite Of Passage Taken Late

196

Storming The Castle

Searching The Six-Fingered Man

Cannot Kill True Love

To The Death, No To The Pain

I Will Always Come For You

197

Ah, Kirk, My Old Friend

It Is Very Cold In Space

I Spit My Last Breath

From Hell's Heart, I Stab At Thee

I've Done Far Worse Than Kill You

198

From Davis To Pope

Driving Fast On Blood Fuel

Roy In A Point Flash

A Collector And Devil

An Inquest Of Da Vinci

199

Forty-Four Hundred

Taken Away From Their Time

Returned Years Later

Altered By The Future Ones

Trying To Salvage The World

200

Jeb Kerman Mun Bound

Approaching Kerbin's First Moon

First Kerbal Landing

Many Explosions Before

He Has Finally Made It

201

On Throne Lexa Sits

Skaikru Joins Coalition

Now The Thirteenth Clan

Rise Of Wanheda Begins

Beginning Of Power Shift

The End

202

Is This The Ending

Hope You Enjoyed These Tanka

Has Been A Journey

Mind And Heart Put Into Words

I Believe Our Time Is Done

ABOUT THE AUTHOR

Born in 1973, Brett C Persson is a poet and recovering alcoholic who crafts his experiences into thought-provoking poetry and prose. As the author of his debut book, "Poetry Of An Addict" and several other collections, Brett hopes to provide readers with poignant insights into the life of an ex-addict as he ranges across universal themes through descriptive wordplay and vivid imagery. He aims to reassure readers who are struggling with alcoholism that they're not alone, helping them find solace in the unique and expressive power of poetry. Brett currently resides in Buckeye, Arizona with his wonderful wife and three daughters.

11/14/11

www.ingramcontent.com/pod-product-compliance
Lightning Source LLC
Chambersburg PA
CBHW050824180626
46814CB00004B/1455